Here's all the great literature in this grade level of *Celebrate Reading!*

BOOK D
My Favorite Foodles

Featured Poets

Eve Merriam
Lucia and James L. Hymes, Jr.
Dennis Lee
John Ciardi
Charlotte Zolotow

Big Book & Little Book

BOOK E
Happy Faces

A DELL YOUNG YEARLING

IT'S GEORGE!

Story by Miriam Cohen
Pictures by Lillian Hoban

Nathaniel Talking
by Eloise Greenfield

illustrated by Jan Spivey Gilchrist

ANN MORRIS
ON THE GO
PHOTOGRAPHS BY KEN HEYMAN

BOOK F
A Canary with Hiccups

Celebrate Reading!
Big Book Bonus

Happy Faces

Titles in This Set

About the Cover Artist
Roni Shepherd painted the animals on the cover.
She has had lots of pets: mice, cats, chickens, and fourteen dogs.
She doesn't have pets now, but she loves to paint happy-faced
animals like those on the cover of this book.

ISBN 0-673-81125-5

1997
Scott, Foresman and Company, Glenview, Illinois

Acknowledgments appear on page 144.

12345678910DR010099989796

Happy Faces

ScottForesman

A Division of HarperCollins*Publishers*

Contents

Nice Mice

My Family

Realistic fiction by Carmen Tafolla

In the Desert

READ
ALONG

Good Friends

Nice Mice

MOUSE'S MARRIAGE

BY JUNKO MORIMOTO

Once, long ago, there lived
an elderly mouse couple.
They had
a very beautiful daughter,
whom they loved very much,
and because she was
their only child,
they wanted her to have
the best and mightiest husband
in the world.

So they set off to find him.

First they asked the Sun.
"We think you are the best
and mightiest in the world,"
they said to the Sun.
"Will you marry
our beautiful daughter?"

The Sun beamed down on them,
but just then . . .

a big fluffy Cloud
passed over the Sun,
covering him up.

"Oh, Cloud,"
said the Mice,
"We think you must be the best
and mightiest in the world.
Will you marry
our beautiful daughter?"

The Cloud nodded wisely,
but just then . . .

the Wind came rushing in
and blew the Cloud
right across the sky.

"Oh, Wind,"
said the Mice,
"We think you must be the best
and mightiest in the world.
Will you marry
our beautiful daughter?"

The Wind blew very hard,
but just then . . .

the Wind was stopped by a Wall.

"Oh, Wall,"
said the Mice,
"We think you must be the best
and mightiest in the world.
Will you marry
our beautiful daughter?"

The Wall smiled down
on the Mice,
but just then . . .

the Wall began to crack.
Out tunneled some Mice.

"Look at that,"
said the parents.
"We Mice are the best
and mightiest of all . . .

Our daughter shall marry a mouse."

And so she did.

WHO
WILL
BELL
THE
CAT?

a play based on Aesop's fable
by Sandy Asher

CHARACTERS

FIRST STORYTELLER

SECOND STORYTELLER

THIRD STORYTELLER

CAT

OLD MOUSE

YOUNG MOUSE

SILLY MOUSE

WISE MOUSE

MICE

FIRST STORYTELLER:	Once there was a cat . . .
CAT:	Meow!
SECOND STORYTELLER:	And some mice . . .
MICE:	Squeak! Squeak! Squeak! Squeak!
THIRD STORYTELLER:	The cat was sneaky.
FIRST STORYTELLER:	He liked to sneak up on the mice.
SECOND STORYTELLER:	He was very quiet.
THIRD STORYTELLER:	By the time the mice heard him . . .
MICE:	Squeak! Squeak! Squeak! Squeak!
FIRST STORYTELLER:	It was too late.
CAT:	Meow!
SECOND STORYTELLER:	The cat always caught the mice.

THIRD STORYTELLER:	The mice didn't like that one bit.
FIRST STORYTELLER:	They called a meeting.
SECOND STORYTELLER:	Old Mouse was the first to speak.
OLD MOUSE:	That cat must be stopped.
YOUNG MOUSE:	I'm afraid of him, Old Mouse.
OLD MOUSE:	I know, Young Mouse. We're all afraid.
SILLY MOUSE:	I'm not. I'm not afraid of anything. Not even the cat.
WISE MOUSE:	Then you are a very silly mouse.
SILLY MOUSE:	No, I'm not. I'm a very brave mouse.
WISE MOUSE:	We'll see, Silly Mouse. We'll see.

OLD MOUSE:	Friends, listen to me. We must stop the cat.
WISE MOUSE:	But how?
OLD MOUSE:	I don't know, Wise Mouse. But we must find a plan.
YOUNG MOUSE:	Why does he always catch us, Old Mouse?
OLD MOUSE:	That's a good question, Young Mouse. It's because we can't hear him.
YOUNG MOUSE:	Why can't we hear him?

OLD MOUSE:	It's because he's so quiet.
SILLY MOUSE:	He's sneaky.
WISE MOUSE:	He never makes a sound.
YOUNG MOUSE:	Can't we make him noisy?
THIRD STORYTELLER:	At first, the other mice laughed at Young Mouse.
MICE:	Squeak! Squeak! Squeak! Squeak!
FIRST STORYTELLER:	Then Silly Mouse got an idea.
SILLY MOUSE:	Let's put a bell on the cat!
OLD MOUSE:	A bell?
SILLY MOUSE:	Yes, a bell! Then every time he moves, the bell will ring.

YOUNG MOUSE:	He'll be noisy!
OLD MOUSE:	And we'll hear him.
YOUNG MOUSE:	Then we can run away.
SILLY MOUSE:	He'll never catch us.
OLD MOUSE:	We don't need to be afraid anymore.
SECOND STORYTELLER:	The mice cheered.
MICE:	Squeak! Squeak! Squeak! Squeak!
THIRD STORYTELLER:	Silly Mouse took a bow and said . . .
SILLY MOUSE:	Thank you.
YOUNG MOUSE:	It's a good plan. Isn't it, Old Mouse?
OLD MOUSE:	Yes, it's a fine plan. Don't you think so, Wise Mouse?

FIRST STORYTELLER: Wise Mouse wasn't sure. She said…

WISE MOUSE: Maybe. Maybe not.

SILLY MOUSE: Maybe not?

OLD MOUSE: Why not?

WISE MOUSE: A bell on the cat would be a good thing. But who will put the bell on the cat?

SECOND STORYTELLER: The mice stopped cheering.

THIRD STORYTELLER: They thought about Wise Mouse's question.

FIRST STORYTELLER: And the cat just waited.

CAT: Meow!

SECOND STORYTELLER: Wise Mouse asked her question again.

WISE MOUSE: Who will bell the cat?

OLD MOUSE: Not I.

YOUNG MOUSE: Not I.

WISE MOUSE: And not I.

SILLY MOUSE: I'll do it. I'm not afraid.

WISE MOUSE: We'll see, Silly Mouse. We'll see.

THIRD STORYTELLER: Silly Mouse got a large bell and a long rope.

FIRST STORYTELLER: He waited until the cat fell asleep.

SECOND STORYTELLER: Then he crept up as quietly as he could.

THIRD STORYTELLER:	But the cat woke up!
CAT:	Meow!
FIRST STORYTELLER:	The other mice tried to warn Silly Mouse. They cried . . .
MICE:	Squeak! Squeak! Squeak! Squeak!
SECOND STORYTELLER:	Silly Mouse dropped the bell.
THIRD STORYTELLER:	Then he ran for his life!
SILLY MOUSE:	I'm back! I've changed my mind! I'm not sure I like this plan.

	The other mice welcomed him home.
MICE:	Squeak! Squeak! Squeak! Squeak!
SECOND STORYTELLER:	Then Wise Mouse said…
WISE MOUSE:	Making a plan can be very nice, but before you try it out, it's wise to think twice.
THIRD STORYTELLER:	And the cat smiled and said…
CAT:	Meow!

The MICE go MARCHING

by Hap Palmer

The mice go marching up the monster, dear, o dear!
The mice go marching up the monster, dear, o dear!
They're stepping softly through his hair
So monster will not know they're there
Oh the mice go marching up the monster, dear!

The monster sneezes suddenly, achoo! achoo!
The monster sneezes suddenly, achoo! achoo!
He shakes and makes a thunderous sound
The mice fly off and tumble down
When the monster sneezes suddenly, achoo!

My Family

MAMA'S BIRTHDAY PRESENT

by Carmen Tafolla

Francisco ran into the garden. His grandmother was reading a book.

"Grandma! Grandma!" called Francisco. "Next Sunday is Mama's birthday! Mama always surprises me with a party for my birthday. Can we surprise Mama with a party?"

"That is a wonderful idea, Francisco," said Grandma. "Today is Monday. If we begin today, we will have seven days to plan a party."

"Mama always gives me a present for my birthday," said Francisco. "What present can I give Mama?"

"I don't know," said Grandma. "But don't worry. We can make a piñata to break. Your mama will enjoy that."

So Grandma and Francisco made a piñata.

On Tuesday, Francisco wondered about Mama's present.

Francisco went to talk with Papa about Mama's birthday party.

"What present can I give Mama?" asked Francisco.

"I don't know," said Papa. "But don't worry. I can play my guitar. Your mama will enjoy that."

So Papa promised Francisco he would play his guitar.

On Wednesday, Francisco wondered about Mama's present.

Francisco and his older brother went to invite Señora Molina to Mama's party. Señora Molina had a tortilla shop.

"What present can I give Mama?" asked Francisco.

"I don't know," said Señora Molina. "But don't worry. I can bring some hot tortillas, fresh off the stove. Your mama will enjoy that."

So Señora Molina promised Francisco she would bring hot tortillas, fresh off the stove.

On Thursday, Francisco wondered about Mama's present. He went to talk to his friend Gina about it.

"What present can I give Mama?" asked Francisco.

"I don't know," said Gina. "But don't worry. We can make confetti eggs to crack on people's heads. Your mama will enjoy that."

So Gina and Francisco filled and painted the bright confetti eggs.

On Friday, Francisco wondered about Mama's present.

So he went to speak to Grandpa Pérez.

"What present can I give Mama?" asked Francisco.

"I don't know," said Grandpa Pérez. "But don't worry. We can make some sweet buñuelos. Your mama will enjoy that."

So Francisco and Grandpa Pérez made some sweet buñuelos.

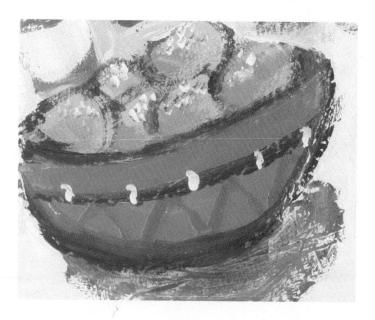

On Saturday, Francisco still wondered about his present for Mama.

But Francisco had many things to do. He helped his brothers and sisters look for a place to hang the piñata.

He talked to Papa about the songs Papa would play on his guitar.

He talked to Señora Molina about the tortillas she would bring.

He found a safe place to hide Gina's confetti eggs and Grandpa Pérez's sweet buñuelos.

Everyone was ready for Mama's surprise.

On Sunday, everyone came to the party. Mama was very surprised.

Papa played his guitar. Señora Molina's hot tortillas smelled wonderful.

Grandpa's sweet buñuelos tasted wonderful.

Everyone ate and sang and had fun. The children cracked confetti eggs over everyone's heads. Then they all lined up to take a swing at the piñata.

Everyone looked happy. Everyone except Francisco.

"Francisco, what is the matter?" asked Mama.

"I did not know what to give you for your birthday, Mama."

"Oh, Francisco," said Mama. "This party was the best present you could give me. No, the second best."

"Second best?" asked Francisco.

"Yes. The best present of all is having my family and friends here with me. That is the most wonderful part of a party!"

Mama gave Francisco a big hug. Then they all took turns hitting the piñata. The one who broke it was Francisco.

And Mama enjoyed that.

In the Desert

Baby Rattlesnake

TOLD BY TᴇATA
RETOLD BY LYNN MORONEY
ILLUSTRATED BY VEG REISBERG

Out in the place where the rattlesnakes lived, there was a little baby rattlesnake who cried all the time because he did not have a rattle.

He said to his mother and father, "I don't know why I don't have a rattle. I'm made just like my brother and sister. How can I be a rattlesnake if I don't have a rattle?"

Mother and Father Rattlesnake said, "You are too young to have a rattle. When you get to be as old as your brother and sister, you will have a rattle, too."

But Baby Rattlesnake did not want to wait.
So he just cried and cried. He shook his tail
and when he couldn't hear a rattle sound,
he cried even louder.

Mother and Father said, "Shhh! Shhh!
Shhhhh!"

Brother and Sister said, "Shhh! Shhh!
Shhhhh!"

But Baby Rattlesnake wouldn't stop crying.

He kept the Rattlesnake People awake
all night.

The next morning, the Rattlesnake
People called a big council. They talked
and they talked just like people do, but
they couldn't decide how to make that
little baby rattlesnake happy. He didn't
want anything else but a rattle.

At last one of the elders said, "Go ahead,
give him a rattle. He's too young and he'll
get into trouble. But let him learn a lesson.
I just want to get some sleep."

So they gave Baby Rattlesnake a rattle.

Baby Rattlesnake loved his rattle.
He shook his tail and for the first time he
heard, "Ch-Ch-Ch! Ch-Ch-Ch!" He was so
excited!

He sang a rattle song, "Ch-Ch-Ch!
Ch-Ch-Ch!"

He danced a rattle dance, "Ch-Ch-Ch!
Ch-Ch-Ch!"

Soon Baby Rattlesnake learned to play tricks
with his rattle. He hid in the rocks and
when the small animals came by, he darted
out rattling, "Ch-Ch-Ch!" "Ch-Ch-Ch!"

He made Jack Rabbit jump.
He made Old Man Turtle jump.
He made Prairie Dog jump.

Each time Baby Rattlesnake laughed and
laughed. He thought it was fun to scare the
animal people.

Mother and Father warned Baby Rattlesnake, "You must not use your rattle in such a way."

Big Brother and Big Sister said, "You are not being careful with your rattle."

The Rattlesnake People told Baby Rattlesnake to stop acting so foolish with his rattle.

Baby Rattlesnake did not listen.

One day, Baby Rattlesnake said to his mother and father, "How will I know a chief's daughter when I see her?"

"Well, she's usually very beautiful and walks with her head held high," said Father.

"And she's very neat in her dress," added Mother.

"Why do you want to know?" asked Father.

"Because I want to scare her!" said Baby Rattlesnake. And he started right off down the path before his mother and father could warn him never to do a thing like that.

The little fellow reached the place where the Indians traveled. He curled himself up on a log and he started rattling. "Chh-Chh-Chh!" He was having a wonderful time.

All of a sudden he saw a beautiful maiden coming toward him from a long way off. She walked with her head held high, and she was very neat in her dress.

"Ah," thought Baby Rattlesnake. "She must be the chief's daughter."

Baby Rattlesnake hid in the rocks. He was excited. This was going to be his best trick.

He waited and waited. The chief's daughter came closer and closer. When she was in just the right spot, he darted out of the rocks.

"Ch-Ch-Ch-Ch-Ch!"

o!" cried the chief's daughter. She whirled around, stepping on Baby Rattlesnake's rattle and crushing it to pieces.

Baby Rattlesnake looked at his beautiful rattle scattered all over the trail. He didn't know what to do.

He took off for home as fast as he could.

With great sobs, he told Mother and Father what had happened. They wiped his tears and gave him big rattlesnake hugs.

For the rest of that day, Baby Rattlesnake stayed safe and snug, close by his rattlesnake family.

From TeAta to You

by Lynn Moroney

I wrote Baby Rattlesnake, but I didn't make up the story. I learned it from a wonderful storyteller named TeAta, who is a member of the Chickasaw Nation. TeAta learned her first stories from her father when she was a little girl. Over the years, she has told her stories to children and adults, kings and queens, and even a president!

Photo/Doug Thurston

Photo: Dean Doerr

Long ago, telling a story was the only way to "pass it on." Now, we can do this through books. I feel very proud to "pass on" this story to you. When you tell or read Baby Rattlesnake to someone, then you will be "passing it on" too…and that is the way of stories!

Lynn Moroney

PINCUSHION CACTUS

by Myra Cohn Livingston

Right at the place
Where our garden begins
There's a cactus all covered
With needles and pins.

It's a very bright green
And as round as a ball,
And the pins and the needles
Are silver and tall.

But you have to be careful
Each time you go through,
Or the cactus will prickle
Like pincushions do.

THE SNAKE IS LONG

by Karla Kuskin

The snake is long
The snake is thin
And every year he sheds his skin.
And every year his skin is new.
I cannot say the same
Can you?

The Desert

by Carol Carrick

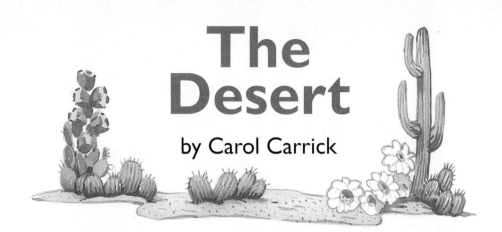

The desert is dry.
It hardly ever rains here.
It is a difficult place for animals to live, but
many animals make their homes in the desert.

Elf owl

Animals need to keep cool in the hot sun.
This tiny owl has made its home in a cactus.
The hole in the cactus was once a
different bird's nest.
Now it is a cool place for the owl to rest.

Animals need food and water to live.
Large animals must live near a water hole.

Coyote

Bobcat

The desert sun is very hot.
So the animals rest in the shade all day,
and hunt at night when it is cool.

Small animals dig into the ground
to stay safe and cool.
Others hide under plants and rocks.
Some animals live far from water.
This pack rat eats seeds and plants.
It gets the water it needs from its food.

Pack rat

Toad

Rattlesnake

These animals are covered with scales.
Scales help keep them from drying out.
This rattlesnake may bite, but it will warn you
first with the rattle in its tail.

This roadrunner has long legs to move fast over the hot ground.
It runs to catch snakes, lizards, and insects for its food.

It is hard to live in the hot, dry desert.
These desert animals know how.

Roadrunner

Horned lizard

Good Friends

40198-4•U.S. $2.95
CAN. $3.95

A DELL YOUNG YEARLING

IT'S GEORGE!

Story by **Miriam Cohen**
Pictures by **Lillian Hoban**

George was writing something.
"What does it say?" he asked Jim.
"I don't know. What *does* it say?"
Jim said.
Anna Maria looked. "It doesn't say
anything, because he can't write.
He is D-U-M," Anna Maria announced.

"So what? He's still good!" said Jim.
"You don't know everything!" Paul said.
But everybody knew that Anna Maria
was the smartest in First Grade.

Some of the kids tried to help George.
"Just do it like this," Jim said.

"Try, man," said Willy and Sammy.
"You can do it!"

But Danny shook his head.
"He'll *never* get it," he said.
And Anna Maria said, "You can't *get*
smart. You just are or you aren't."

But George was better than anybody at
taking care of the class hamster.
It never bit him.

And he always fed the fish just the
right amount.

One day everybody was working on
projects. Jim and Paul were doing
"The Worst Dinosaur! Tyrannosaurus Rex!"

Margaret and Sara were making up math
puzzles. Louie was drawing a map of a city.
And Anna Maria was writing a book
with chapters.

George was working by himself on a secret project. The secret was that he couldn't think of a project.

"Danny, why don't you work with George?"
the teacher said.

"I want to work with Sammy," Danny said.
And he ran to Sammy's table.

The next day, George did not come to
school. Just before lunch, the principal
came in.

"I have a big surprise for First Grade.
To find out what it is, you will have to
watch Channel 3 at four o'clock
this afternoon."

After school, Jim and Paul went to Jim's house, and Jim's mother made them popcorn to eat.

At four o'clock, the news came on.
The announcer said, "Good afternoon.
This is News 3 at Four.

"A little boy in our city leaves his house
early every morning, so that on his way to
school he can visit with a friend of his
who lives alone.

"That friend is 79-year-old
Henry Emmons. Every morning Henry
and his young friend sit on the front
porch, rock in their chairs, and wave at
the people driving to work.

"But let's go to that front porch, where our reporter, Angela Simms, is talking to that little boy. He is six-and-a-half-year-old George Jenkins."

"It's George!" Jim and Paul yelled.

The reporter was saying, "Tell us what happened this morning, George."
"Mr. Emmons fell down off the rocker and closed his eyes. I tried to make him get up, but he wouldn't."

"And then what happened, George?"
"I called 911 on the telephone. I told them
  Mr. Emmons was sick, and they should
  come to his house."

"And the Rescue Squad did come, didn't
it George? It came in time to save
Mr. Emmons, who is feeling much better,
thanks to his smart young friend.

"Thank you, George. Now, back to
News 3 at Four."

The next morning, at a special assembly
for the whole school, the principal made
a speech about George.

"This young man knew just the right thing to do. He saved his friend's life."

All the kids and the teacher were smacking
George on the back and hugging him.

Then a reporter came to take George's picture for the newspaper. Anna Maria stood next to George. "He's in *my* class," she said.

The reporter put George and the whole
First Grade in front of the school flag.
"Hold it! Smile!"

And the picture in the paper showed
George and all his friends looking happy
and proud.

IT'S LILLIAN HOBAN!

Photo: Mary Eastman

I enjoyed drawing the pictures for It's George! because I got to draw children feeling surprised, happy, and even angry. Best of all, I like to draw children who are happy.

I liked drawing Anna Maria and George being photographed for the newspaper. I wanted to show how proud Anna Maria is of George. That's why I drew her arm around him. You can tell Anna Maria doesn't think George is D-U-M now!

Lillian Hoban

MAKING FRIENDS

by Eloise Greenfield

when I was in kindergarten
this new girl came in our class one day
and the teacher told her to sit beside me
and I didn't know what to say
so I wiggled my nose and made my bunny face

and she laughed
then she puffed out her cheeks
and she made a funny face
and I laughed
so then
we were friends

Books to Enjoy

Peter's Chair
by Ezra Jack Keats

Peter's parents painted
all of his baby things pink
for his new baby sister.
But they forgot Peter's
chair! See what
Peter does.

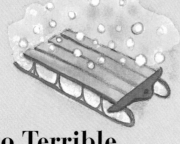

Two Terrible Frights
by Jim Aylesworth
Illustrations by
Eileen Christelow

A little girl and a little
mouse try to get a
bedtime snack. They
both get a big
surprise instead!

Frog and Toad All Year
by Arnold Lobel

Do you have a best
friend? Frog and Toad
are best friends. They
have lots of fun when
they're together.

Grandpa's Garden Lunch
by Judith Caseley

Can Sarah and her grandpa really eat the garden they grew for lunch? Find out!

Nature's Footprints in the Desert
by Q. L. Pearce and W. J. Pearce
Illustrations by Delana Bettoli

Many animals live in the desert. Follow the footprints in this book to meet them.

Mouse's Birthday
by Jane Yolen
Illustrations by Bruce Degen

Mouse's house is very small. His friends are big so they have quite a squeeze.

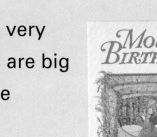

Glossary

Words from your stories

Aa

announcer

An **announcer** tells you things on the radio or television, and at ball games or other contests. **announcers**

Bb

bell

A **bell** makes a ringing sound. Some **bells** make a pretty sound when you shake them. **bells**

best

His work is good. Your work is better. Her work is **best.**

Cc

cactus

A **cactus** is a plant that grows in hot, dry places. **Cactuses** are covered with sharp points.
cactuses

cry

Cry means to have tears come from the eyes. Babies **cry** when they are hungry. cried, crying

Dd

daughter

A girl is the **daughter** of her father and mother. The Smiths have four **daughters**. daughters

desert

A **desert** is a place without water or trees. **Deserts** are usually hot and sandy. deserts

Ee

enjoy

To **enjoy** means to be happy with. The children **enjoyed** their visit to the park. enjoyed, enjoying

Ff

first

First means coming before all others. The **first** letter of the alphabet is A. Ann sang **first.**

Gg

grade

A **grade** is a year of study in school. She is in the first **grade.** grades

Hh

happen

Happen means to take place. What **happened** at the party? happened, happening

Ii

idea

An **idea** is a thought or plan. It was my **idea** to sell lemonade.

ideas

Ll

live

Live means to make your home in a place. We **live** in a big city.

lived, living

Mm

marry

Marry means to become someone's husband or wife. They plan to be **married** in June.

married, marrying

mighty

To be **mighty** is to have great power.

mightier, mightiest

Pp

party

A **party** is a group of people having a good time. Alex went to the birthday **party. parties**

plan

A **plan** is something you have thought about and will do. We have a **plan** for the party. **plans**

principal

A **principal** is a person who is the head of a school. The **principal** of our school is Mrs. Adams. **principals**

Qq

quiet

Quiet means not noisy. Peter was **quiet** when he came home. **quieter, quietest**

Rr

rattlesnake

A **rattlesnake** is a large snake with a broad head. **Rattlesnakes** make buzzing sounds with rattles at the ends of their tails. rattlesnakes

roadrunner

A **roadrunner** is a bird that lives in the desert. **Roadrunners** can run very fast. roadrunners

Tt

tail

A **tail** is the part of an animal's body farthest from its head. A fox has a furry **tail.** tails

Ww

world

The **world** is the Earth and everything on it. Someday I want to travel around the **world.**

ACKNOWLEDGMENTS

Text

Page 10: From *Mouse's Marriage* adapted by Anne Bower Ingram, illustrated by Junko Morimoto. Copyright © 1985 by Anne Bower Ingram for adaptation. Copyright © 1985 by Junko Morimoto for illustrations. Used by permission of Viking Penguin, a division of Penguin Books USA Inc.

Page 34: *Who Will Bell the Cat?* by Sandy Asher. Copyright © 1991 by Sandy Asher.

Page 46: From "The Mice Go Marching" from *Rhythms on Parade.* Words and music by Hap Palmer. Copyright © 1989 Hap-Pal Music. Reprinted by permission of Hap-Pal Music, Inc.

Page 50: *Mama's Birthday Present* by Carmen Tafolla. Copyright © 1991 by Carmen Tafolla.

Page 64: *Baby Rattlesnake* reprinted by permission of GRM Associates, Inc. Agents for Children's Book Press from the book *Baby Rattlesnake,* told by TeAta, adapted by Lynn Moroney, illustrated by Veg Reisberg. Story copyright © 1989 by Lynn Moroney. Illustrations copyright © 1989 by Veg Reisberg.

Page 92: "From TeAta to You" by Lynn Moroney. Copyright © 1991 by Lynn Moroney.

Page 94: "Pincushion Cactus" by Myra Cohn Livingston. From *Whispers and Other Poems* by Myra Cohn Livingston. copyright © 1958 by Myra Cohn Livingston, copyright © renewed 1986. Reprinted by permission of Marian Reiner and the author.

Page 95: Text from "The Snake Is Long" from *Roar and More* by Karla Kuskin. Copyright © 1956 by Karla Kuskin. Reprinted by permission of HarperCollins Publishers.

Page 96: *The Desert* by Carol Carrick. Copyright © 1991 by Carol Carrick.

Page 104: *It's George!* Story by Miriam Cohen. Pictures by Lillian Hoban. Text copyright © 1988 by Miriam Cohen. Illustrations copyright © 1988 by Lillian Hoban. Published by Greenwillow Books, a Division of William Morrow & Company, Inc. Reprinted by permission of William Morrow and Company, Inc.

Page 133: "It's Lillian Hoban!" by Lillian Hoban. Copyright © 1991 by Lillian Hoban.

Page 134: "Making Friends" from *Nathaniel Talking* by Eloise Greenfield. Text copyright © 1988 by Eloise Greenfield. Illustrations © 1988 by Jan Spivey Gilchrist. Reprinted by permission of Marie Brown Associates.

Artists

Illustrations owned and copyrighted by the illustrator.
Roni Shepherd, cover, 1–9, 48–49, 62–63, 102–103, 136–143
Junko Morimoto, 10–33
Pamela Rossi, Set Design and Masks, 36–45
Krystyna Stasiak, 46–47
Kelly Stribling Sutherland, 50–61
Veg Reisberg, 64–91
Helen Cowcher, 94–95
Joe Veno, 96–101
Lillian Hoban, 104–132
Jan Spivey Gilchrist, 134–135

Freelance Photography

Pages 36–45: Tom Lindfors

Photographs

Pages 34–35: Barbara Reed and John Williams
Page 92: Doug Thurston (Courtesy of Lynn Moroney.)
Page 93: Dean Doerr (Courtesy of Lynn Moroney.)
Page 133: Mary Eastman (Courtesy of Lillian Hoban.)

Glossary

The contents of the Glossary have been adapted from *My First Picture Dictionary,* copyright © 1990 Scott, Foresman and Company; *My Second Picture Dictionary,* copyright © 1990 Scott, Foresman and Company; and *Beginning Dictionary,* copyright © 1993 Scott, Foresman and Company.